LAKE OF SKULLS

A KNIGHT'S STORY

by Paul Stewart and Chris Riddell

Atheneum Books for Young Readers

New York   London   Toronto   Sydney

Atheneum Books for Young Readers
An imprint of Simon & Schuster Children's Publishing Division
1230 Avenue of the Americas
New York, New York 10020
Copyright © 2003
by Paul Stewart and Chris Riddell
First published in Great Britain in 2003 by
Hodder Children's Books, a division of Hodder Headline Limited
Book design by Tom Daly
The text for this book is set in Cheltenham.
The illustrations for this book are rendered in pen, brush, and ink.
Manufactured in the United States of America
First U.S. edition, 2004
2 4 6 8 10 9 7 5 3 1
Library of Congress Cataloging-in-Publication Data
Stewart, Paul, 1955-
Lake of Skulls / Paul Stewart and Chris Riddell.— 1st U.S. ed.
p. cm.
Summary: An unbonded knight traveling as a "free lance" meets more
than his share of trouble when he signs on with Lord Big Nose to
recover a crown from the Lake of Skulls.
ISBN 0-689-87239-9
[1. Knights and knighthood—Fiction. 2. Adventure and
adventurers—Fiction.] I. Riddell, Chris. II. Title.
PZ7.S84975Fre 2004
[Fic]—dc22   2003027208

For William and Joseph

ONE

"Hey, you!"

I looked up. I was in this flyblown, two-bit tavern, drinking watered-down cider. All of a sudden a heavy great tankard came whistling toward me. I ducked.

Cider slopped all down my front as, cursing under my breath, I looked round to see the tankard slam into the face of the timid-looking drinker next to me. It struck his jaw with a sound like a hammer splintering wood.

With a low groan he slumped to the floor at my feet. His drink—spiced cider, if the sickly smell was anything to go by—joined the cider down my front. I was a mess. But not as much of a mess as the little fellow. Two teeth lay on the floor in front of him. A trickle of blood oozed out over the sawdust.

Behind me, a loud, beastlike roar went up. I turned to see a great hulk of a man—all hairy jowls and heaving gut—lumbering from leg to leg in a slow battle jig. I recognized him at once.

His fists were clenched. His bloodshot eyes were wild.

"Come on, if you think you're hard enough!" he was bellowing.

Here we go again! I thought. Why do I always seem to end up in this type of a place? You'd think I'd have learned by now. All I'd wanted was a quiet drink. Was that too much to ask? Was it?

Given the day I'd had so far, maybe it was. . . .

◆ ◆ ◆

I'd woken that morning, bitten to blazes. The night before, Jed and I had taken shelter from a storm in a dilapidated stable. By the early morning light, I saw that the whole place was jumping.

'Course, Jed was all right. Fleas hadn't touched him. Too busy gorging on yours truly. As I scratched at the bites, Jed neighed. I could have sworn he was laughing.

I packed up, saddled up, and crept out of there, as quiet as a princess breaking wind. This far out in the back of beyond, it didn't pay to draw attention to yourself.

Normally I stick to the castle tournaments, but after the season I'd just had, I was prepared to do anything: exhibition

matches, sword displays, even village-green jousts. I wasn't proud.

I'd knocked over my fair share of big-time knights at the beginning of the year, but a churned-up tournament field and a second-rate lance that had shattered in my hand had spelled disaster. After that particular tumble, I'd been laid up for a month—and the shoulder injury still hurt when it was cold. . . .

I'd ended up in the Badlands, where every group of rundown hovels boasted a robber baron, and the contests were—how shall I say?—less refined.

It was another beautiful Badlands' day. Murky, gray, and so cold it felt like someone jabbing needles into your skin. The sky was the color of stale gruel, and by late morning an icy drizzle had begun to fall. I felt the familiar twinge in my shoulder.

I'd heard talk of a contest in a village up ahead, near a mountain lake, and fancied Jed's and my chances against some yokel on a donkey.

Sure enough, just the other side of a scrubby thornwood, was a miserable collection of ramshackle dwellings clustered round one of those low, mud-brick halls that pass for manor houses in these parts. Jed and I went down the muddy main street. There wasn't a villager to be seen.

Jed whinnied and reared up, nostrils quivering. I steadied him, told him it was all right—but he had a point. The place stank. The kind of smell that clings to you like a landlady on payday. But then, that's village life for you—all cabbage water and open sewers. Give me a life on the road any day.

I soon solved the mystery of the missing villagers. They were all standing outside the ropes of a makeshift

tournament ring, set up on a muddy
patch of grass on the far side of the
manor house.

My heart sank. The actual tournament

was nothing more than a wooden club-
and-shield contest, winner takes all. Two
hefty oafs were at the center of the ring,
battering each other for all they were

11

worth. Blood and sweat spattered the cheering onlookers. Above them, on a raised platform, sat a sour-faced character with a big nose, shifty eyes, and heavy, fur-lined robes—no doubt the lord of the rundown manor and everything else round.

I'd seen his type a hundred times before. Little men with big ideas who'd arrive one day with a purse of gold and a gang of thugs. A promise here and a threat there, and pretty soon they were running the place and putting on all sorts of airs and graces.

Nothing like hosting a tournament to make a man feel like a real lord.

Lord Big Nose caught my eye. "Well, well, well. Look what we have here," he called across, his voice thin and wheedling. "If it isn't a real-life knight come to take part in our humble contest. How about hand-to-hand combat on foot, sir knight?"

"Jousting's more my area of expertise," I shouted back.

Just then one of the competitors took a blow to the throat and a chop to the back of the neck. He thudded to the ground like a sack of turnips, down for the count, and was dragged away by the heels. The winner grinned toothlessly and raised his club as the crowd cheered. I turned away.

"You must have traveled far," came the wheedling voice. "Are you quite sure you wouldn't like to take part?"

I looked back to see a fresh contender climbing into the ring. Big, hairy, and ugly he was, a great hulk with a face that wouldn't have looked out of place on a vegetable stall: shapeless as a potato and with two great cauliflower ears. His eyes narrowed. "Hey, pretty boy," he grunted. "Fancy your chances?"

I shook my head. Swordplay was one thing—I could have filleted Potato Head here like a fat moat fish with a few sweeps of my sword. I might have been desperate for money—but not *that* desperate. Club fighting is strictly for mugs.

As I climbed back into the saddle, the crowd roared with approval as some poor sap was pushed into the ring. I didn't hang around to watch the fight. I already knew the outcome.

Pausing only briefly to hammer a loose nail back into one of Jed's rear hooves, I left the village. I hoped the horseshoe would hold till I could get him re-shod. That's the thing about being a free lance—no lord to pay your upkeep. Mind you, I'd tried that once. It hadn't worked out.

That said, it's a good life if you like clean sheets, regular meals, the best armor money can buy—and a pompous, overfed lord ordering you around morning, noon, and night. Of course, it doesn't help when his ladyship falls in love with you! Things got pretty complicated.

I ended up break-
ing her heart,
and his nose—
and had to
swim the castle
moat at mid-
night to avoid
a permanent
stay in the
dungeons.

No, bonded life was not for me. Even though I could have made it big, I wasn't prepared to become some pampered lord's pet knight again. I would just have to hope that Jed—an Arbuthnot thoroughbred gray—didn't end up lame.

By now, the drizzle had turned to a cold, driving rain that numbed the fingers, dulled the mind, and played havoc with my shoulder. What was more, I was hungry. My stomach was grumbling like a courtier with corns, and Jed was complaining even louder. The nail had come loose. He was beginning to limp. There was no choice; I had to go back.

"It's all right, boy," I said. "We'll go back and get you taken care of. Find a place for the night. Fresh straw for you, clean sheets for me. And to hell with the expense."

Jed didn't need telling twice. Without so much as a twitch on the reins, he turned and trotted back toward the village.

It was getting dark by the time we hit town for the second time. The grinning blacksmith robbed me blind, but Jed was happy to be in a warm stall for the night. For myself, I'd noticed a warm glow and the sound of laughter coming from a tavern by the green. I left the blacksmith's and headed for it.

Inside the place was buzzing. I recognized one or two characters from the tournament arena—a hefty man with a black mustache and a swollen, bloody nose; a short, pudgy-faced individual I'd seen getting pummeled in the ring, a dirty bandage round his head . . .

Suddenly, standing in front of me, was a tall woman with hair the color of spun gold and a smile that was brighter than a summer morning. She looked me up and

down—and clearly liked what she saw.

"The name's Nell," she said, flashing me that dazzling smile. "I run this place."

"Pleased to meet you, Nell," I said, smiling back.

"Likewise, sir knight, I'm sure," she said shyly. "What can I get you?"

I told her I was looking for a good meal and a warm bed for the night. She could offer both—though at a price that made Jed's stall seem like a bargain. That's the trouble with being a knight, I thought, as Nell disappeared into the kitchen. You look wealthier than you are and everyone robs you blind. Maybe I should find it flattering.

While I was waiting for my meal, I stepped up to the bar and ordered a large cider. I licked my lips in anticipation as the barman poured the bubbling brown liquid from barrel to tankard.

"Thirsty work, knighting and all," said my neighbor—the timid-looking one.

I nodded. The barman pushed the tankard across the bar. I seized it, raised it to my lips, and was just about to drink when a rough voice cut through the friendly babble.

"Hey, you!"

So there I was, in this flyblown, two-bit tavern, cider down my front, the timid-looking drinker—jaw stoved in by a tankard—at my feet, and a great potato-headed oaf lumbering toward me.

"It's you, isn't it?" he bellowed, his face coming so close to mine I was struck by his stinking breath. "Isn't it?" he repeated. "You're that fancy, pretty-boy knight."

"I am a knight," I said, calmly and slowly, meeting his gaze. "Unbonded. A free lance . . ."

The tavern fell still. Potato Head turned to address his cronies. "An unbonded knight, if you please," he mocked. "A free lance. Very posh." An edge came into his voice. "Unbonded vagabond, more like! A freeloader!"

An ominous rumble went round. I could tell that they thought Potato Head had a point. It was time he and I had a little chat.

I pushed my face into his and (trying hard to ignore the cabbage breath) told him exactly what I thought of his manners—punctuating my comments with a series of heavy punches to the stomach.

As he bent over double, I moved to one side and drove a well-aimed boot into his great backside. He went sprawling, cracking his jaw on the floor where he landed.

The crowd fell silent. Then one of them laughed. Then another. Soon, the whole lot of them were cackling like ferrets in a feather quilt.

Potato Head rolled over, rubbed his jaw, and climbed to his feet. He kicked the still unconscious little fellow viciously in the ribs.

The crowd booed.

"Yeah?" Potato Head sneered as he looked round. "What are you going to do about it, eh?"

The crowd fell still once more. I stepped forward. "How about this?"

I punched him. A swift jab to his jaw. He didn't know what hit him. I punched him again—a punishing hook to the head.

His neck jerked backward. His eyes dimmed. But he didn't fall over.

I'd seen this before. A great hulk, too stupid to know when to drop.

The crowd remained silent as I raised a single finger and prodded him in the chest.

Potato Head grunted, twisted, and fell to the floor with a loud thud and a flurry of sawdust.

The crowd went wild.

Just then, the kitchen door flew open and Nell burst in, demanding to know what was going on. The crowd, a fickle bunch, nodded toward yours truly. Nell strode round to the front of the bar.

She looked at the timid drinker just coming round. She looked at Potato Head out cold. She put two and two together and came up with five.

"I'll have no troublemakers in my inn,"

she told me, her green eyes flashing with anger. "Get out!"

I didn't argue. By the way she was fussing over Potato Head—loosening his tunic

and patting
his head—it was
obvious whose side
she was on. He was a
local. I was a stranger.
End of story.

LaSalle Academy Media Center

I turned to go. At that moment, a thin, wheedling voice broke through the silence.

"Not so fast."

I turned and looked up into the upper gallery. Leaning over the balcony was the big-nosed, sour-faced lord in the fur-lined robes I'd seen at the tournament.

"We meet again, sir knight." He raised an eyebrow. "You handle yourself well," he said,

nodding down at Potato Head. "You've defeated our champion here."

Out of the corner of my eye, I could see Nell pouting.

"You and I should talk," Lord Big Nose said. "Nell, refill our guest's tankard."

I knew what was about to come. "Not interested," I said, and turned to go.

Behind me, I heard Lord Big Nose chuckle unpleasantly. He clicked his fingers. Instantly, three armed stooges appeared from the shadows, crossbows raised and pointed in my direction. I turned back. A triumphant smile was playing over his lordship's thin lips.

"Maybe I will have that drink after all," I said.

THREE

"You could be just the person I'm looking for," his lordship was saying, as I tucked into the meal Nell had finally served up.

I nodded, mid-spoonful of stew, but said nothing. The pair of us were seated opposite each other at his table in the upper gallery. Below us, the tavern was rowdy. It was as though nothing had happened—and that's the way I liked it. Unfortunately Lord Big Nose wasn't about to let me forget.

"I liked the way you took care of yourself down there," he told me.

"The bigger they come, the harder
they fall," I murmured.

"That was why I organized the contest
this afternoon," he went on. "To find
someone to carry out a little job for me.
Someone tough, fearless—who knows
how to take care of himself . . ."

It was clear I wasn't going to be

allowed to finish my meal in peace. I laid my spoon down.

"'Course, I'd make it worth your while," he continued. "And I can see from your armor and weapons that you could do with a piece of gold or two—not to mention that old nag you rode into town on."

That riled me. Jed might not be as young as he once was, but he was a thoroughbred Arbuthnot warhorse through and through. Normally I would have put old Big Nose right on a few points. But with the crossbows still glinting in the shadows, I knew this was neither the time nor the place to discuss horse breeding. I sat back in my chair and folded my arms.

"So, what's the deal?" I said.

39

His words buzzed round inside my head like horseflies in a stable. I'd heard it all before. The promise of easy money. The offer of good lodgings and better feasting. The flattering claim that, for a man like me, the task should be simpler than herald duty at a banquet.

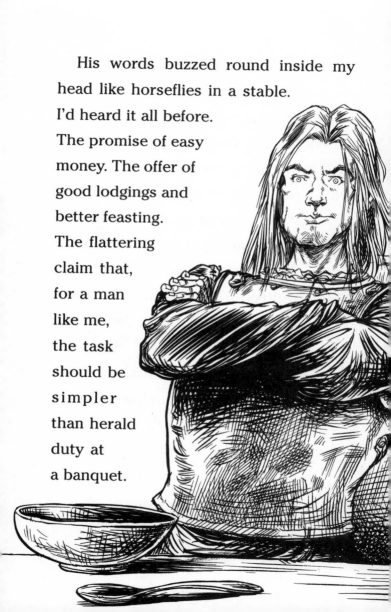

A pack of lies, of course, every word of it.

Trouble was, it was the end of the tournament season—and a lousy one at that. Of course, if I were a bound knight, I'd winter up in some castle or other, perfecting my swordplay and honing my lancing skills on a quintain. But I'm a free lance. There'd be no cozy castle for me this winter. I'd be lucky if the meager amount I'd earned this season saw me through to the new year.

I stared back at the narrow, shifty eyes in front of me. Sickening though it was, Lord Big Nose was looking like my one hope. What was more, though I didn't like to admit it, he was right. The whole thing did sound right up my alley.

This was the deal. There was an island. Craggy, misty, stuck in the middle of a lake in the mountains. The Lake of Skulls. That was where he wanted me to go.

There, I'd find a huge pile of skulls. (The clue was in the name.) My job was to climb up to the very top, where I'd find the skull of an ancient king still wearing his golden crown. I had to take the crown and return with it to Lord Big Nose, whereupon he'd cough up a purse full of gold crowns, and free cider and board for the whole winter.

I could tell by the way he licked his lips greedily when he mentioned it, that this crown meant a lot to him. Why he didn't simply go and get it himself, who knows? Probably believed the place was cursed or something. Superstitious lot, these Badlands yokels.

Anyway, I wasn't asking questions. Lord Big Nose might well be a sniveling,

odious little man with more money than sense, but he needed my services and I needed his money, and that—I'm sorry to say—is the way of the world these days. Besides, how difficult could the job be?

I was about to find out. . . .

FOUR

I finished off my meal, mopping up the greasy remains of the stew with a hunk of bread. Lord Big Nose was still going on about the crown, saying how it really wasn't worth very much at all, but that it had sentimental value. He clearly didn't want me to know how much it meant to him.

I smiled and nodded in what I hoped were all the right places, but, to be honest,

I wasn't really listening. I was thinking about Jed.

Obviously, I wouldn't be able to take him with me. I didn't fancy leaving him tethered up by the edge of the lake, and taking him over to the island wasn't an option. I didn't want to risk losing my most valuable possession in a night swim in some icy mountain lake—and rowboats and horses are not a good combination. I knew I had no other choice but to stable him up in the village until my return.

"So it's settled then," said his lordship, climbing to his feet and smiling that simpering smile of his. "Let's shake on it."

I gripped his outstretched hand. It was like shaking hands with a dead fish.

"Bring the crown to my manor," he told me, "and I'll have your money waiting for you.

"Good luck, sir knight—I trust you'll leave at once."

With that, he turned and left, with the troll-like retinue of bodyguards and armed henchmen clumping down the stairs after him.

I snorted. If Big Nose thought I was about to set off on his little quest in the middle of the night, he had another thing coming. I'd booked a bed for the night, and I was going to get good use out of it. I scraped the chair back and headed upstairs.

My room was small and dingy, and I banged my head on a low beam. But the bed had clean linen on it, and the mattress was soft. *Very* soft . . .

I woke up to the sound of barrels clanking below my window. The sun was already up. Cursing myself for oversleeping, I jumped up, splashed water over my face, and headed downstairs. Nell was in the bar, a mop in her hands and a bucket at her feet. She flashed me

one of her dazzling smiles. There were obviously no hard feelings.

"Sleep well?" she said brightly.

I told her I had. Despite, or maybe because of the blow to my head, I'd slept like a log. Now it was time to set off. Turning down her offer of breakfast, I settled up and headed for the blacksmith's.

Jed was happy to see me. He nuzzled against me as I untethered him, and blew billowy clouds of warm air on my hands. He hated it when we were separated, and I felt a twinge of guilt that I was going to have to leave him behind all over again. Still, I had no other option.

The blacksmith directed me to some stables on the outskirts of the village. They were rundown,

shabby buildings, but the half-dozen horses in the battered stalls looked well-groomed and content. Jed was less sure.

As I slipped down from the saddle, he reared up and pounded the air with his front hooves.

"Frisky, ain't he?" came a voice.

I turned to see a thin, weasel-featured man, all darting eyes and twitchy side-whiskers. He reached up and,

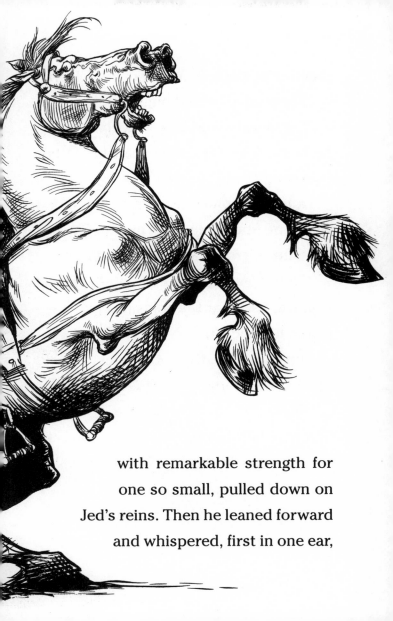

with remarkable strength for
one so small, pulled down on
Jed's reins. Then he leaned forward
and whispered, first in one ear,

then the other. Jed quivered and fell still.

"Impressive," I told him.

"I've always had a way with horses," he said. "Like my father, and his father before him."

I knew I'd come to the right place. Jed would be fine while I was away. I handed over three groats as a down payment.

"So, where are you heading?" Weasel Features asked as the coins jangled down inside his pocket.

"Just up into the mountains," I said coolly. "Not horse country."

"Don't tell me," he said, drawing in breath noisily through his teeth, "the Lake of Skulls, I'll be bound. To retrieve that accursed crown."

He shuddered. I listened closely.

"We locals know when to leave well enough alone," he told me. "It doesn't do to go stirring things up at the lake. It's an ancient place, full of ancient things—and should be respected, if you ask me. But it's no good telling his lordship that. Oh, no. He just wants that crown and doesn't care how he gets it—or what trouble he causes. 'Course, too lily-livered to

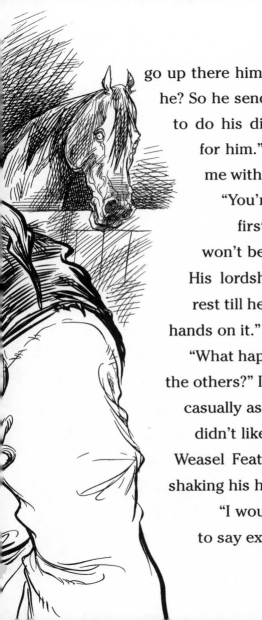

go up there himself, isn't he? So he sends others to do his dirty work for him." He fixed me with his eyes. "You're not the first and you won't be the last. His lordship won't rest till he's got his hands on it."

"What happened to the others?" I asked as casually as I could. I didn't like the way Weasel Features was shaking his head.

"I wouldn't like to say exactly," he

said, and pointed at the stalls. "But put it this way, not one of them has ever come back for his horse."

"Don't worry, Jed, old boy," I said, patting his flank. "I'm not planning on being a footslogger for any longer than I have to."

I tried to sound relaxed, but I had to admit I was beginning to get a bad feeling in the pit of my stomach. Perhaps it was too much cider. Or perhaps it was the look old Weasel Features had; the look of someone who thought he'd just inherited a thoroughbred Arbuthnot charger—and three groats in the bargain.

"Tell me," I said, slipping another groat from my pocket. "What exactly do you know about the Lake of Skulls?"

◆ ◆ ◆

I knew, from Lord Big Nose's instructions, that the lake lay on the far side of the vast pine forest to the northeast of the village. He'd failed to mention how close the trees were packed together and how dense the undergrowth was. With my sword drawn, I hacked my way through.

But it was slow going. Just as well I'd left Jed behind.

As I battled on, I mulled over Weasel Features's far-fetched tale—a tale of an ancient king who fell in love with an enchantress and made her his queen. The poor sap discovered that his beloved and her hand-maids were dabbling in the dark arts. He had *them* banished, and *her* executed—

but not before he'd forced her to make him an enchanted crown that was meant to make him top dog around these parts.

But something went wrong. Who knows what? According to the legend, though, the king's head now sits on a pile of skulls in the center of the island, still wearing the enchanted crown—a band of gold in the shape of a coiled serpent, with the words of the queen's spell engraved around it.

Nice touch, I thought. I smiled to myself as I remembered old Weasel Features reciting it reverently.

"He who wears the serpent's band,
Shall be dreaded throughout the land;
Destined to be raised up on high,
And worshiped till the lake runs dry."

I chuckled. No wonder it had got Lord Big Nose all excited. It was amazing what some people chose to believe. Mind you, so long as there was the promise of a purse full of gold, I wasn't complaining.

It was dark inside the forest, and by the time I finally reached the other end, I found it was dark outside as well. The sun had set and the fat yellow moon was just dragging itself up over the horizon. It shone across the rippled water of the vast mountain lake before me. Peering ahead through a thin mist that

hung over the water, I could just make out the island in the middle.

I marked the place where I'd emerged from the forest with a rock so I could follow my own path back, and set off along

the lakeside. I soon came to a rickety wooden jetty. Tied up at the end—just as old Big Nose had promised it would be—was a coracle.

I stepped in. The small boat rocked from side to side. I sat down smartly. The last thing I wanted was to fall in—and if you've ever attempted the crawl in a breastplate and leg armor, you'll know why. I've seen stones swim better!

The moon was higher now and I could see the island clearly. It didn't look too far away. I untied the mooring rope, picked up the paddle, and pushed off from the jetty.

I've never liked coracles. I mean, don't get me wrong. They're fine for fat abbots who want to do a spot of fishing. But if you actually want to get anywhere, forget it! A horse trough would be quicker.

It took ages for me to get into a steady forward rhythm—by which time the wind had got up, a thick mist was coiling off the choppy water, and the moon kept

disappearing behind the clouds. I'm not the superstitious type, but believe me, there was something evil about the place. It made my flesh creep.

I thought I'd feel better when I got across the lake.

I thought wrong.

FIVE

The island was a mass of giant black boulders, slippery and covered with moss. Just landing the coracle was a feat in itself. When I finally managed to scramble ashore onto a cold, slimy rock, my hands were grazed and my knees battered black and blue.

The wind had grown stronger, and the whole place was filled with moans and sighs as it howled through the gaps between the boulders. No wonder the island had a reputation among the Badlands yokels. I might be a tournament knight from the castle belt, but when it came to the Lake of Skulls, I was beginning to see their point.

I started to climb. If I could reach the top of the jumble of huge rocks, I'd be able to get my bearings. That is, if I didn't break my neck first. And all the while, the wind howled, and the mist coiled, and the moon- light came and went. . . .

Finally, panting like a friar's donkey, I reached the

top and sank to my knees. It was a while before I got my breath back and was in any state to take in my surroundings.

I was on a plateau of rock, as flat as an out-of-tune minstrel. Just then, the moon burst out from behind a passing cloud. It shone down on a tall stack of what looked like large white rocks, not a hundred yards in front of me.

I headed toward it, hoping the moon would stay shining long enough for me to get there.

The howling grew louder. The mist coiled round my legs, my chest, my head. It tasted stale, like a mouthful of yesterday's cider. The only good thing was that the moon kept shining.

Then, as the stack loomed up in front of me, I wished it wasn't.

The white rocks were glaring at me. Each and every one. They weren't rocks at all. They were skulls. Hundreds of skulls, piled up high, one on top of the other— and at the very top, there it was.

The skull with the gold crown.

It wasn't a nice feeling meeting the black gaze of thousands of skulls, but, that aside, perhaps Lord Big Nose was

right after all. Perhaps this was a routine job. I wouldn't have minded a bit more of a challenge. But then, after the season I'd had, I reckoned I was due a lucky break.

I started up the pile of skulls. They shifted beneath my feet, skull knocking against skull with every step. Halfway up, the toe of my boot caught in an eye socket. I stumbled and almost fell back. As I grabbed hold of the skull above me to steady myself, its jawbone came away in my hand. It's a good thing I'm not squeamish. But then, as I always say, it's the living that do you harm, not the dead.

Then again, as I climbed higher and higher, the way the color of the skulls turned from brown to yellow to gleaming white was certainly unnerving. Those at the bottom must have been there for

decades, centuries even. Closer to the
top, some of them looked a little too
recent for my liking.

One of the skulls had scraps of hair still attached. Another had bits of tattered skin clinging to the bone. . . .

I thought of the horses in Weasel Features's stable. Perhaps I was looking at their owners.

I was near the top of the skull mountain, the crown almost within my grasp at last. I reached for the serpent-like band of gold. The skulls creaked and cracked beneath my feet as my fingertips grazed the glittering scales of the crown.

Just a little bit farther!

My grip closed round the crown. I lifted it as gently as I could. The crown came free. So did the skull.

Slipping from the top, it bounced down the pile of skulls—making a sound like a lame horse on cobblestones— all the way down to the bottom where, with an echoing thud, it landed on the rocks below. It lay there, grinning up at me.

The next instant, an ear-splitting screech shattered the stillness of the misty night air. For a moment, I imagined it was the skull. But only for a moment.

Below me, something big, hairy, and, by the sound of that screech, pretty angry, was heading this way. As it approached the foot of the skull mountain in long, loping strides, it threw back its head and shot me a look of pure, venomous hatred.

I could hardly believe my eyes. It was the biggest, hairiest hag I'd ever seen, all foul, matted hair and snarling fangs. She was big. She was ugly. And getting bigger and uglier the closer she got. Grasping the crown tightly, I skidded and jumped my way down the far side of the mound of skulls and set off across the rocks.

The hag screeched with rage. A blood-chilling noise, a cross between a wounded bear and a roaring furnace.

I tucked
the crown into
my belt and headed
for a tall rock to my
right. Then, ducking
down out of sight
behind it, I struck
off to my left. That
was the way I'd
climbed up. With
a bit of luck, if I
kept my head down,
the swirling mist and shifting moonlight
would keep me hidden while I clambered

back down again. I'd be in that coracle and away before you could say . . .

"Hell's teeth!" I yelled, stopping in my tracks.

The hag must have taken a shortcut across the rocks. Now she was standing in front of me, blocking my path.

She grinned at me, her slavering teeth glinting as she tossed a razor-sharp scythe from hand to hand. She nodded toward the crown.

I smiled back. "Nothing personal," I said. The hag's face betrayed no sign of understanding. "I'm just doing a favor for a lord I know. Perhaps you've heard of him—little chap, big nose . . ."

Without warning, the hag lunged forward, her face contorted with rage. I drew my sword as she swung her evil-looking scythe. There was a screaming clash of metal as the weapons struck one another, and a violent jolt that juddered through my entire body, knocking me off balance and sending me tumbling backward.

The hag bellowed and slashed at me with her scythe as I flapped out of the way like a freshly landed pike. The blade nicked my shoulder, too close for comfort. I could smell her fetid breath as she closed in for the kill.

I slid round on the greasy surface of the rock and used an old jousting trick I hadn't tried since I was a squire—the Jester's Gambit; a standing back flip with trailing sword arm—straight over the hag's head.

My sword met with resistance. I heard a

gasp and a gurgle and the sound of the scythe clattering down onto the rocks beside me as I landed.

At the same moment, a cloud passed and the moonlight streamed down brighter than ever. I found myself staring at the hag before me. Her eyes glinted, her teeth gleamed. There was blood, black as pitch, pouring down her front—but I knew I had to make sure. The last time I'd failed to finish off a wounded attacker, I'd almost paid the ultimate price. I wasn't about to make the same mistake again.

With a grunt of effort, I pulled my sword free and, double-handed, swung it through the air. The blade

whistled. For a moment, the hag remained standing. The next, she collapsed—her body falling one way; her head, the other.

And I was out of there, faster than a hound on a boar hunt. By the time I arrived back at the coracle, I was wet with sweat and panting like a dog. I'd done it. I'd retrieved the crown, and slain the creature who had been guarding it in the bargain. Now all I needed to do was get it back to Lord Big Nose and claim my fee. I'd never been so pleased to see a coracle before in my life.

I climbed down into it. The worst, I thought to myself, is over.

Little did I know that the worst was still to come.

SIX

As I pushed out into the choppy waters of the lake, the coracle bucked beneath me like an unbroken jousting pony. Then, as I reached down for the paddle, I saw it.

Huge it was, gnarled and hairy, with lake water glistening on its knuckles—a monstrous great hand that gripped the side of the boat.

Quick as an eel, I grabbed the paddle and smashed it down

on the grasping fingers. The coracle lurched wildly. The hand let go and slid beneath the water.

I drew my sword and searched the murky depths for the hand's owner— although, truth be told, I already had an idea of who that might be. . . .

Suddenly, there was a splash and I felt a vicelike grip fasten round my ankle. Before I knew it, I was dragged off my feet and into the icy water. I swallowed a

lungful before I remembered to close my mouth. I was sinking like a castle cat in a sack of stones. As I said before, armor and water don't mix.

The next instant, I felt two gigantic hands close round my throat. They held on tight.

As my eyes cleared for a moment, I saw that—just as I'd feared—my assailant was a second hag. She was older, stronger, and twice as big as the first, though with a definite family resemblance, if her ugly mug was anything to go by. It wasn't only the size and power that made her so dangerous, but the fact that she was clearly out for revenge. I had killed her sister. From the look in those bloodshot eyes, I knew that this one was personal.

The water boiled as the pair of us

thrashed about. I was desperate to break the hag's lethal grip—and she was just as desperate to hang on.

I twisted and writhed, I kicked and punched, but even when my blows struck their target, the hag held on firmly. She wouldn't be satisfied until she had squeezed the last drop of life out of me.

My lungs were burning, and there was a ringing in my ears. Any moment now, I was going to black out. I knew I had to do something—and fast!

Abruptly, I let my body go completely limp. My feet grazed the bottom of the lake, my arms dropped to my side. I closed my eyes.

The hag's grip seemed to tighten, then gradually relax.

We rose to the surface—me, clamped under one of her huge arms, limp as a strangled newt. As we surfaced, the hag gulped down huge lungfuls of air, while I snatched tiny, silent breaths and played dead for all I was worth.

Slowly, cautiously, I closed my hand around the handle of the knife at my belt. The hag waded ashore and climbed up onto a boulder, still clutching me tightly. Then she let me go. I dropped, with a thud, onto the cold rock.

And there I lay, motionless, like a turbot on a serving platter, not moving so much as a muscle. I was good. Very good.

The hag bent down and sniffed at me closely, her wet, matted hair brushing my face. She looked me over, up and down, before settling on my right leg.

She lifted it with one great paw and pulled off my shin guard with the other. Then, delicately, she rolled back my stocking, and looked at my bare shin the way a glutton eyes a leg of pork.

She licked her lips; she bared her yellow

fangs. The stench of her breath was vile. I sprang up and, with one sharp, punching thrust, drove the blade of my knife into the hag's heart.

A look of bewilderment flickered across her face as she staggered backward. She let out a low gurgling sound,

deep in her throat. She coughed. She spluttered. Blood trickled down from the sides of her mouth as she collapsed and slowly rolled off the boulder, back into the water.

The Lake of Skulls fell still.

With the crown hanging from my belt, I retrieved the upturned coracle. Thankfully it hadn't drifted off. I turned it over, climbed in, and started paddling for the second time.

It was only when I got halfway across the lake that I paused to look back. Far behind me was the pile of skulls, still gleaming in the moonlight. I snorted. To think that, as I'd reached up for the crown, I'd wished for a bit more of a challenge. Well, that would teach me!

Just then, the water boiled to my left. It was probably just a carp or a pike. But I wasn't hanging around to find out. Seizing the paddle with both hands, I raced across the lake faster than a jester with his tights on fire.

By the time I reached the jetty, I was dripping with sweat. Every muscle in my body was knotted with exertion. I climbed back onto dry land, my legs wobbling beneath me.

To be honest, I'd have liked to rest up for a while. But the greater the distance between me and the Lake of Skulls the better, and just then I was still too close.

I pressed on.

SEVEN

It wasn't long before I came to the rock
marker. I made my way back down the
path I'd cut through the forest. It should
have been easier going but, cold,
exhausted, and half choked to death, I
made heavy weather of it. To make mat-
ters worse, I was soaked to the skin and
my armor was beginning to play up.

My hacketon squelched, the heavy
sleeves feeling stiff and unyielding. My
schynbalds groaned with every step I

took. And as for the rerebraces on my arms; they were on the verge of seizing up completely.

I tried to think of something else—the warm, soft bed back at the tavern, for instance. But it was no good. And as I trudged on, the mattress of soft pine needles beneath my feet began to look more and more inviting.

I told myself to get a grip; to pull myself together. One night on a feather bed and I was going soft. Besides, there was something else urging me on. The thought of Lord Big Nose. I couldn't wait to see the look of surprise on his smug,

arrogant face when I handed over the crown—and the pain when he handed me my fee.

Day was breaking by the time the trees began to thin out. I found myself back on a narrow track that led into the village. I pushed the crown behind my breastplate to conceal it from prying eyes, and set off.

My first stop would be the stables, to check on Jed. As I

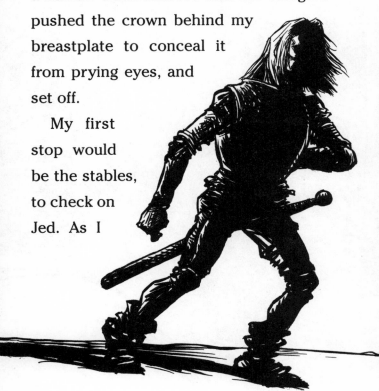

drew close, I could hear voices coming from inside. Two voices. One belonged to Weasel Features—nasal, high-pitched. The other was deeper, rougher.

They were in the middle of some deal or other. I was immediately suspicious.

"Twenty gold sovereigns," Gravel Voice was saying, "if you throw in the Arbuthnot."

"You drive a hard bargain, so you do," Weasel Features whined. "Still, needs must . . . twenty gold pieces, it is."

I strode forward. "Not so fast," I said.

Weasel Features spun round. His face fell. "You," he said. "I didn't think you'd be back."

"Sorry to disappoint you," I said, "but I've come for my horse. Big, gray Arbuthnot, goes by the name of Jed—or had you forgotten?"

"The Arbuthnot's yours?" said Gravel Voice, looking downcast.

"That's right, slimeball," I said. "And he's not for sale."

I untethered Jed and led him from the stall. Then I mounted up, turned back, and flicked two groats toward old Weasel Features. They landed in the straw at his feet.

"What I owe you," I told him. "Oh, and you can go ahead and sell those other horses," I added. "Their owners won't be back. Trust me."

I flicked the reins and we were off.

Weasel Features called out, "Did you find it, then? Did you find the serpent crown?"

I made no reply. That was for me to know and him to wonder. My next stop was Lord Big Nose's rundown manor house. I'd save the explanations till then.

♦ ♦ ♦

The low sun cast long shadows across the track. The sky was pink. Bad weather was on its way. I passed the tournament green and was turning at the tavern, when I heard a familiar voice call out.

"You're back, brave sir knight! I was afraid I'd seen the last of you." It was Nell the tavern keeper, her voice soft and tender.

"I didn't know you cared." I smiled, reining in Jed.

"Oh, sir knight, of course I do," She tossed her golden hair off her shoulders. "You look tired. Come inside and have a drink. I've got a place by the fire, just for you."

"You have?" I said. She'd really got my attention now.

"Of course. And, sir knight," she went on, "I'd be honored if you'd let me join you." She fluttered her big, green eyes at me.

"Well, just a quick cider, maybe," I said, dismounting.

Jed neighed angrily and stamped his foot as I tied him up. I followed Nell toward the tavern.

"Not that way," she said as I made for the front entrance. "Here. This is the door for my special guests."

She motioned me through a small side entrance inside. It was dark and warm. A fire flickered in a grate and a large chair and table with a full tankard waited for me.

"Help yourself," Nell said softly, closing the door behind me.

I was about to reply, when I was beaten to it by a gruff voice behind me.

"Don't mind if I do," it said.

Before I could look round, I heard a strange rustling sound, followed by a low hiss. I felt my head explode.

Everything went white, then black.

Then, nothing.

EIGHT

I was awakened by the feel of something warm and wet sliding across my forehead and down my cheek. For a terrifying moment, I thought I was back on the island, and that one of the hags had come back to finish me off.

My eyes snapped open—to see Jed standing beside me. His neck was lowered and he was licking my face.

"Jed," I murmured as I looked up into his soft, furry face. "What happened?"

Jed whinnied and scraped his hoof on the ground. I pulled myself up, and winced as a bolt of pain shot through my skull and down my spine. I looked round.

I was back in the stables, sharing a stall with Jed. How had I got there? I asked myself, the pain now a dull throbbing ache at the back of my head.

"Awake, are you?" came a familiar voice. It was Weasel Features, bowl and cloth in hand, standing in front of me. "Found you in the gutter outside the tavern." He cackled. "Blind drunk, so Nell said. Had to throw you out, by all accounts."

"Nell!" I cursed, and my hands flew to my breastplate. The crown was, of course, gone.

"Still, it was the least I could do after you were so obliging about the little business with your horse here—even making up the sum you owed me. . . ."

"Yes, yes," I said, trying to clear my head. "Don't mention it. How long have I been out?"

"Oh, I found you this morning at sunup, and it's now . . ." He squinted past my shoulder at the patch of sky in the window. "Almost sundown."

I groaned and brushed the straw from my shoulders. "Look after Jed for me," I told Weasel Features. "I'll be back before morning. And try not to sell him while I'm gone!"

I left, with Weasel Features still cackling at my little joke.

◆ ◆ ◆

The noise coming from the tavern as I drew closer was as rowdy and loud as ever. There was raucous laughter and the babble of conversation; there was the clinking of tankards and the shifting of chairs; and behind it all, the sound of a fiddle, flute, and tabor playing stomping reels.

I stepped up to the door and walked in.

Every eye in the place turned toward me. The laughter and conversation ceased. The band stopped playing. There's nothing like a friendly welcome, I thought—and this was *nothing* like a friendly welcome.

I heard a voice from behind me. "Nasty bump you've got there, stranger."

I turned. It was Nell. She was smiling, but not pleasantly. It was then that I noticed the character beside her, a hefty hand resting on her shoulder. Potato Head. As our eyes met, he grinned. Again, it wasn't pleasant.

"You want to be careful who you pick fights with, pretty boy," he said.

Just then, a second voice addressed me, calling down from the gallery. Lord Big Nose. "Sir knight," he said, "I'm afraid you are too late."

I looked up. He was leaning against

the balustrade, a smug expression on his face and the gold serpentlike crown on his head. In the shadows behind him were his henchmen, their crossbows primed.

"As you can see, our champion here has beaten you to it," he said, and glanced down at Potato Head, who patted the bulging leather money pouch tied to his belt. "But thank you so much for all your trouble." Lord Big Nose smirked. "Better luck next time, eh?"

I knew when I was beaten. You had to in my line of work. Lord Big Nose up there didn't care how he got his creepy serpent crown. And as for old Potato Head, he was just doing what came naturally. No, it was Nell I was disappointed in.

"Nothing personal, you understand," she said.

I nodded. I'm sure she meant it. Certainly it was galling to have gotten so far only to have been caught off-guard in a moment of carelessness, but then that was the risk every free lance had to take.

"No bad feelings, then," she said. "Have a tankard of cider before you leave. On the house." There was something in her voice that suggested she felt bad about tricking me. I hoped so.

"All right," I said at last. "Make it a large one!"

"Don't push your luck," Nell said, pointedly picking up a small tankard. Perhaps she didn't feel so bad after all. I shrugged and, ignoring Potato Head's sneers, took my drink to the far corner.

Soon, the conversations were struck up once again, drinking was resumed, the musicians began playing—and everyone seemed to forget about me altogether. Which was just as well, as I didn't feel much like chatting.

Lord Big Nose was holding court up in the balcony, talking loudly about how he was now going to rule the world. No

one could resist him now that he wore the serpent crown. And those Badlands yokels cheered his every word.

I had another drink.

Maybe it was the whack on the head, maybe it was the cider or the heat from the open fire, but pretty soon I nodded off. When I awoke, the roaring log fire had turned to smoldering embers, and

there were snoring bodies everywhere. I'd clearly missed one heck of a party.

It was high time I left. I made my way across the room, trying not to step on the bodies on the floor, when one of them turned over and mumbled in his sleep, "Pretty-boy knight."

It was Potato Head. He was dead to the world after what looked like a barrel or three of cider. A smile played over his lips. Clearly, he was enjoying his dream.

I bent down and untied the leather thong attached to his belt. The heavy purse fell into my hand.

"Pleasant dreams," I murmured as I pocketed the gold—and Potato Head gave a contented grunt. I smirked. He'd be smiling on the other side of his face when he woke up.

Turning to leave, I felt something wet hit my cheek. I looked up at the balcony. Lord Big Nose was slumped over his table. I could see his fur-lined shoulders outlined against the open window.

Passed out and spilled his wine, I thought. Just another petty tyrant with big ideas and no head for drink.

I left and headed back to the stables.

Jed whinnied softly when I appeared. He was as pleased as I was to be leaving this godforsaken Badlands' hole at last. I quickly unhitched the rope, climbed into the saddle, and took up the reins.

We headed back up the main street, past the tavern, and out of town. As we approached the crossroads, a dark figure darted across our path and Jed reared up in fright.

I fought with the reins and finally managed to calm him down. It wasn't like Jed to be so easily spooked—but then I didn't blame him. My own heart was racing, and a cold, clammy sweat clung to me.

"Steady, Jed," I said, as I reined him back. "We can take it easier now."

Jed whinnied, and I wiped the sweat from my face. I looked at my hand. It was stained red with blood—blood that wasn't mine.

I remembered the tavern, Lord Big Nose slumped at the table, the spilled wine dripping from the balcony onto my face—only, I now realized with a jolt, it wasn't wine.

He who wears the serpent's band,
Shall be dreaded throughout the land;
Destined to be raised up on high,
And worshiped till the lake runs dry.

Suddenly it all fell into place, and I could visualize the whole appalling scene.

The headless body of Lord Big Nose slumped by the open window. The third monstrous hag returning to the Lake of Skulls and placing a fresh head wearing the serpent's band on top of the pile of skulls.

Lord Big Nose would be worshiped all right—and feared and dreaded. But not in quite the way he thought.

I hadn't liked Lord Big Nose, not from the first moment I'd laid eyes on him, but that didn't stop me from feeling a pang of pity for the poor, deluded sap. No one deserved that fate. Then again, one thing was for sure: The villagers would be a lot better off without him.

I still don't believe in magical crowns and elixirs of eternal life. That kind of stuff's for fairy tales. No, if there's anything that this little escapade has taught me, it's this:

Be careful what you wish for, because you might just get it.

It was good advice. I only hoped that I'd be able to stick to it myself. With the thought of Lord Big Nose fresh in my mind, it shouldn't be difficult.

Then again, as a free lance—dependent on the whims of others—anything was possible. This time I'd survived, and with a pouch of money that should see me through the barren winter months. Next time, I might not be so lucky.

It was all so uncertain. And yet, in a way, I guess that's exactly what I like about this way of life. The thrill of the chase. The head rush of battle. Dicing with death. Call me a fool, but despite everything, I'm not about to give up being a free lance.

At least, not just yet.

AND HERE'S A BIT OF THE ACTION FROM FREE LANCE'S NEXT ADVENTURE:

FIELD OF BLOOD

A KNIGHT'S STORY 2

Yes, it felt good to be back at a major castle tournament. And from the moment her ladyship's silver handkerchief fluttered down from her snow-white fingers, Jed and I were at it nonstop.

A field-of-silver joust is a straightforward affair. All you have to do is knock your opponent from the saddle. After a slow start Jed and I got into our stride, and knights, large and small, were soon dropping to the ground like bishops in buttered slippers.

The second day went even better. I pitched knight after fine noble knight off their mounts, sending them flying to the ground. By now the crowd was getting excited. The bets were flying, and a lot of people were making a lot of money on yours truly.

But not me. I wouldn't see a brass penny unless I made it to the semifinals.

On the third day, things got tougher. Now it was a gold handkerchief dropping from her ladyship's fingers that got the tournament underway.

A field-of-gold joust is one where, after the unseating, the knights engage in hand-to-hand combat until one or the other gives up. It can get pretty nasty, but the crowds love it.

I got the boastful customer with the snarling boar's head crest in the first round. He went down hard, breaking his leg in three places—and wasn't boasting anymore.

Next up was the showman knight, and I knew I had trouble on my hands. I unseated him on our first charge, but he sprang back to his feet like a foxhound with its tail on fire. The crowd roared as he set about me with his broadsword.

I bided my time, taking what he was dishing out, because I knew his sort— can't resist playing to the crowd and trying one clever move too many. Sure enough, it wasn't long before Showman danced past me with a disguised right-hand slice—and I had him! A swift shield uppercut and a short, sharp body-blow, and the show was over.

Later, back in my tent, Wormrick fussed about my injuries. With a bit of luck, there was nothing that a bit of strapping wouldn't see to. I was through to the semifinals, and as Wormrick finished with me and went off to see to Jed, I pictured the opponent who awaited me the next day.

Hengist was his name—a great brute of a fellow, bonded to the castle, and always clad in dull gray armor. He was as hard as nails and had a grim reputation for fighting dirty.

In the other semifinal, the rich kid with the black warhorse had made it through with a series of spectacular jousts. He was up against the blue knight—a mysterious character who kept his visor down and his thoughts to himself—who'd won through with a series of lucky victories, and nobody rated his chances highly.

Unlike me. All the smart money was being placed on yours truly winning outright. . . .

Just then, the tent flaps opened and in walked the duke of the Western Marches himself. I'd seen him watching the events from the royal throne and noticed the glint in his eyes as he'd won bet after bet on me winning. Close up, he was fatter than I'd thought and, with his pointed yellow teeth and flapping ermine cloak, looked like nothing so much as an overfed wolfhound.

"You seem to be doing well," he barked. "People will make a lot of money if you defeat Hengist."

I nodded, taking his words for a compliment. I should have known better.

"But you're not going to do that," he said sharply.

"I'm not?" I said.

"No, you're going to lose," he said. His jagged teeth glinted in the lamplight. "But make sure you lose convincingly. No one must suspect a thing. . . ."

"And why would I do this?" I asked.

An unpleasant smile spread across Lord Wolfhound's fat face. "Here's a purse of thirty gold pieces for you now," he said, "and there's thirty more later, when you've taken a tumble."

"And if I don't?" I said.

His yellow eyes narrowed. "Then I shall be forced to tell the herald that your documents are forged. You'll be thrown out on your ear." He sneered. "And don't think I couldn't."

I didn't doubt it for a moment.

"It's a good offer," said the duke. "An offer you can't refuse."

"No," I said. "I don't suppose I can."

So there I was, slumped in my chair, my head spinning.

Duke Wolfhound wanted me to throw the joust! Me, Free Lance, throw a joust! I've never thrown a joust in my life! Not that the offer wasn't tempting. I'd make more by losing the tournament than I would by winning it.

And as a free lance, that sort of money wasn't to be sniffed at. Then again, there was the matter of honor. Even if no one ever discovered what I had done, *I* would know . . .

Just then, the tent flaps opened a second time, and a tall, slim figure dressed in a long hooded cape stepped in.

"We must speak at once, sir knight," came a voice—a woman's voice. "It is a matter of the utmost urgency."

Paul Stewart is the author of a number of books for children, including *The Weather Witch*. In addition, his longtime collaboration with illustrator Chris Riddell has produced sensations like *Muddle Earth,* the Blobheads series, and the best-selling Edge Chronicles series. He lives with his wife and two children in Brighton, England.

Chris Riddell's illustrations have graced the pages of many children's books, including *Pirate Diary,* for which he was awarded the Kate Greenaway Medal. He is also an acclaimed cartoonist for Britain's *Observer*. He lives with his wife and three children in England.